The Passion of Martin Fissel-Bran‹

La Passion

Martin

Fissel-R

Translated by Melanie Kemp

With an introduction by Brian Evenson

Christian Gailly

The Passion
of Martin
Fissel-Brandt

University of Nebraska Press : Lincoln and London

Publication of this translation was assisted by a
grant from the French Ministry of Culture–
National Center for the Book.
Originally published as *La Passion de Martin Fissel-
Brandt*. Copyright © Editions Minuit, 1999
Translation and introduction copyright ©
2002 by the University of Nebraska Press. All
rights reserved. Manufactured in the United
States of America. ⊚

Library of Congress Cataloging-in-Publication-Data
    Gailly, Christian, 1943–
[Passion de Martin Fissel-Brandt. English]
    The passion of Martin Fissel-Brandt / Christian Gailly;
translated by Melanie Kemp.
        p.cm. ISBN 0-8032-2180-0 (cloth: alkaline paper) –
ISBN 0-8032-7097-6 (paperback: alkaline paper)
        1. Kemp, Melanie, 1970– II. Title.
PQ2667.A354 P3713 2002 843'.914–dc21 2001027707

Contents

I would first like to thank my family, my two beautiful sons and my husband, Dan Kemp, for having put up with me this past year. Thank you, Dan, for the countless hours you spent with me suggesting the right sentence structures and for your continued support and love. I would like to thank Christian Gailly for his help and contributions, as well as Jordan Stump, without whom I would never have taken on such a project, nor would I have continued without his encouragement. My thanks also go out to Brian Evenson for his intelligent introduction and corrections and to Warren Motte for his helpful suggestions.

Lurching from one artistic medium to another, the term
"minimalism" has had a somewhat awkward history.
First used in regard to the visual and plastic arts, the con-
cept suggested that by removing possibilities, by strip-
ping away tools and gestures, one might be able to come
closer to an essence (though artists would quickly call the
notion of "essence" itself into question). Minimalist visual art tended to be geometrical, abstract, depersonified.
As Warren Motte suggests, minimalists in the visual arts
relied on "a literal, nonreferential objecthood rather than
any form of representational illusion."[1] In music, minimalism refers to the work of Steve Reich and Philip Glass,
among others, who favor applying techniques of iteration
to material that has already been restricted. While visual
minimalism focuses spatially on the nonreferential object, minimalism in music is concerned with employing
limited material over a time continuum to develop a
structure of repetition.

Where the term becomes trickiest is in regard to literature,
particularly American literature. The term minimalism
has been used, often in derogatory fashion, to describe
(and often dismiss) writers who came to prominence in
the 1970s, many of them under the influence of Gordon
Lish (who served as a fiction editor first at Esquire magazine and later at Alfred A. Knopf). These writers, many of

whom resist the appellation, include Raymond Carver, Mary Robison, Amy Hempel, and Bobbie Ann Mason. In Carver's case (and perhaps not exclusively for Carver) a minimalist style was at least partly inflicted: Lish edited Carver's first two books of stories quite heavily, often cutting the stories to half or less of their original length, removing connections, creating gaps, neutralizing dialogue tags, scaling back outward expressions of emotion, and so on.[2] Carver's post-Lish work was more expansive, and Carver himself spoke pejoratively of the term minimalism: "I don't like being called a minimalist writer. . . . Nor do I like the appellation 'minimalism.' It's useless. It was a French critic, in fact, in his review of *What We Talk about When We Talk about Love* for the *Partisan Review*, who called my work 'minimalist.' He meant it as a compliment, but certain critics and reviewers picked it up and used it to start hammering on some writers. I think the sooner such labels go away, the better."[3]

Carver's dismissal of minimalism is perhaps partly due to feeling that what made his early work worthy of the term were Gordon Lish's edits. Carver fears that the edits that might make a story minimalist might dehumanize it. As he says of "Neighbors," one of his stories that Lish edited substantially, "My only fear is that it is too thin, too elliptical and subtle, too inhuman."[4]

In the United States, there has also been a confusion of minimalism with "dirty realism," a term used to designate the writing of figures such as Tobias Wolff, Raymond Carver, and Richard Ford. With Wolff and Carver also being associated with minimalism, the confusion is understandable. Carver, for instance, speaks of the importance of "a return to realism" and "real concerns."[5] As a result, however, minimalism has been seen as having as much to do with content as with technique, the term designating realistic stories about characters who are down and out, members of the lower middle class living gritty lives. Minimalism is thus often regarded as a largely working-class phenomenon. It is this confusion as well that allows Kim Herzinger to suggest that minimalism is realist and regional.[6]

As a result of this confusion, of the simultaneous connection and antipathy between minimalism and dirty realism, minimalism has become a vague term standing for something both easy to hate and easy to dismiss. Indeed, literary critics most often define minimalism as a negative term, seeing the restraint of minimalism as a defect. Very few contemporary American writers would feel comfortable being referred to as minimalist. To repeat Carver, "I think the sooner such labels go away, the better."[7]

*

With American minimalism currently languishing, I think it makes sense to look elsewhere. It is for that reason that translation of Christian Gailly's work is something to be taken seriously not just by those interested in French literature, but by those interested in American writing as well.

France has long had a minimalist tradition. Certainly the lack of affect that writers such as Kim Herzinger see as a primary characteristic of American minimalism has a precursor in the blank writing of Albert Camus's The Stranger.[8] Furthermore, most of the techniques that are tied to minimalism can be traced to Samuel Beckett, who made a decision to write in French "parce qu'en français c'est plus facile d'écrire sans style" (because in French it's easier to write without style). Indeed, Beckett manages to use, in various works, essentially all the stylistic devices that might be seen as defining minimalism.[9]

But Beckett and Camus are historical figures, or at least sufficiently historical as to be dead. What does France have to offer American literature now?

I would argue, a great deal. Writers such as Marie Redonnet, Annie Ernaux, Jean-Philippe Toussaint, Christian Oster, and Christian Gailly offer highly individual approaches that demand a reconsideration of minimalism and its possibilities. The publication of Christian Gailly's *The Passion of Martin Fissel-Brandt* continues the effort of University of Nebraska Press, begun with Jordan Stump's lively translations of Marie Redonnet's fiction, to make a different sort of minimalism available to American readers and writers, a Continental minimalism that is not caught up in a confusion with dirty realism.

The Passion of Martin Fissel-Brandt is Gailly's ninth novel, and his first to be translated into English. Like much of Gailly's work, *The Passion of Martin Fissel-Brandt* is written in short, sharp chapters, in the third person, the novel moving back and forth in time and space from chapter to chapter. The shifts between chapters give a great deal of satisfaction and texture to the narrative, and they allow Gailly to complicate a relatively straightforward tale while forefronting style.

All of Gailly's work is characterized by a fascination with coincidence, with often fantastic chance encounter. Indeed, in Gailly's fiction plot is attenuated into a series of encounters and near encounters. In *Les Fleurs* (1993; The flowers), for instance, the action takes place in little more than an hour. The plot can be easily summarized: A woman travels from the suburbs into Paris by train to meet with a professor. At the same time, a man boards the train, traveling to Paris to meet a friend. They happen to sit next to each other, each registering the presence of the other. As they arrive in Paris, they find that they are each pursuing the same path, until at last they both enter the same apartment building.

Under such circumstances, the rules of life seem to have changed, things seem to be happening for a reason, and even the most banal gestures gain meaning. Gailly manages to make even the simplest incident, the simplest act, such as finding a button or putting on a bandage, a compelling ritual. In L'Incident (1996; The incident), a man's accidental discovery of a purse leads him into a serious obsession with the woman who owns the purse — a single chance encounter (and this with an object rather than with a person) rearranging his life. This focus on a potential but not yet — and perhaps never to be — actualized couple constantly occurs in Gailly's work. Indeed, the condition of being alone and seeking connection seems the lot of nearly all of Gailly's primary characters.

Gailly's work borrows structurally from music, its patterns of fictional repetition and permutation modeled upon musical patterns. In Be-Bop (1995) Gailly uses jazz, and indeed his narrator realizes that his descriptions of jazz might be used to describe his narrative as well: "with blanks, notes, blanks, notes, a little like this book began."

Dring (1991) borrows structurally from a specific piece of music, the Goldberg Variations, offering resounding motifs, characters, objects, and sentence structures that attempt to render music on the page. *K. 622* (1989), arguably Gailly's most disturbing and most impressive work, takes its lead from the Mozart concerto designated by the title. In *The Passion of Martin Fissel-Brandt*, too, one of the characters suggests that "the space on the paper is the space of an orchestra" (chapter 14). Though the character is speaking of her own art, she might equally be speaking of Gailly's.

Part of the reason Gailly's work is so intriguing is because of this structural connection to music. Gailly's characters seem compelled to play certain parts, as though they were instruments in an ensemble. They seem at once people with individual wills and functions of a larger music. Free will and control are constantly in tension.

In *The Passion of Martin Fissel-Brandt*, a series of coincidences carries the titular character on a quest from France across Asia in search of a former lover, the woman who has left him for reasons that become clear only as the narrative develops. The initial catalyst in this case is a bird that has managed to infiltrate the house Martin has rented for a week. As he tries to shoo it outside, a painting tilts. When Martin straightens the painting back into place, he uncovers a letter, which starts him on his quest. At each stage of his journey, his quest is potentially thwartable, but always something unlikely occurs to carry him forward, and he finds his quest enabled rather than hindered, each coincidence stacked precariously on top of the previous. They are, in a sense, unbelievable, as Martin himself realizes when he thinks of telling a coworker about only the first several coincidences: "The twist of fate. She'd never believe me" (chapter 10). At one point, Fissel-Brandt faints, overwhelmed by the sheer weight of coincidence. As a result, he is not killed — his fainting has, quite coincidentally, saved his life.

That Gailly can get away with a proliferation of improbable coincidences is amazing in and of itself. A large part of the reason he can do so stems from his willingness to manipulate style, to acknowledge and accept artifice while still propelling his narrative forward. Indeed, Gailly manages to strike a successful balance between formal experimentation and conventional narration — we can still hear and enjoy the music of artifice and thus allow him a certain playfulness in regard to the mimetic qualities of the text. Even though Gailly's narratives can be roughly classified as realistic, they contain elements that most realisms would exclude. Many of Gailly's books, for instance, offer what I have referred to elsewhere as a "perforated narrative" — a narrative still of a piece but shot through with tiny holes, through which the strange gleams of artifice and style shine. One sees both the representation and the devices that allow that representation to come into being. The risk is that the perforations will distract the reader from the narrative proper, but the balance Gailly strikes is an effective one. The interest of Gailly's narrative lies as much in its idiosyncracies and slight interruptions as in the spooling forth of any semblance of plot.

In *The Passion of Martin Fissel-Brandt*, Gailly offers clipped, terse sentences that seem notational and are often fragmentary. Though they always end with periods, as if they were complete, they are often left unfinished. For instance, one chapter ends: "Slowly, indeed, but, when he entered" (chapter 2). We only discover what happened "when he entered" in the chapter that follows. The narrative voice thus seems at times to suffer from a speech defect. The result is a reading experience that forces the reader to parse language one way and then reparse it to make meaning.

Gailly's work often offers as well a protruding narrator. Largely operating in third person, he nonetheless cannot resist commenting on the act of writing the story. At one point in *Les Fleurs*, for instance, the narrator suggests, "I nearly cut out this passage and then in the end I left it in." This element allies Gailly's writing with metafiction, though his style as a whole still expresses the best of the sparse, minimalist tradition. Indeed, Gailly is a welcome antidote to the split between minimalism and metafiction that has developed in American literature; his work provides the means of prying minimalism away from realism, dirty or otherwise. Though subtle and often mixed into the perceptions of the characters, this protruding narrator is nonetheless present and important in *The Passion of Martin Fissel-Brandt*.

Just as things seem to be beginning, just as the two primary characters meet again, *The Passion of Martin Fissel-Brandt* ends. The narrative is truncated, Gailly thwarting expectations. Yet this is not the blank ending that we find so often in a Carver story or in other American minimalist work. Rather, it is an ending with extreme satisfaction. Indeed, Gailly terminates Martin's quest with a simple and very unsentimental verbal exchange between him and his ex-lover, gathering into this basic interaction the profound opening up of one character to another.

Thus, we have "real concerns" without being encumbered by Carver's cry for "a return to realism." Though Gailly will never generate the horde of followers that Carver has generated, his voice provides an important corrective. He allows us to reconsider minimalism, to separate it out from realism and its subsidiary concerns and to see it in a fresh light. Taken in conjunction with American minimalists and other sorts of writers concerned with style, Gailly's work suggests that there is more space for minimalism to explore and that the mode, if revitalized by work from outside of the United States, can still be dynamic, revelatory, and transformative.

Brian Evenson

NOTES

1 Warren Motte, *Small Worlds: Minimalism in Contemporary French Literature* (Lincoln: University of Nebraska Press, 1999), 9.

2 Based on manuscript evidence from the Lilly Library in Bloomington, Indiana, whose Lish archive contains Carver's manuscripts with Lish's marks on them.

3 David Applefield and Raymond Carver, "Fiction and America: Raymond Carver," in *Conversations with Raymond Carver*, ed. Marshall Bruce Gentry and William L. Stull (Jackson: University Press of Mississippi, 1990), 206.

4 Raymond Carver, "On 'Neighbors,'" in *No Heroics, Please* (New York: Vintage, 1992), 104.

5 Applefield and Carver, "Fiction and America," 207.

6 Kim Herzinger, "Minimalism as Postmodernism: Some Introductory Notes," *New Orleans Review* 16, 3 (1989): 73–81.

7 Applefield and Carver, "Fiction and America," 206.

8 Herzinger, "Minimalism as Postmodernism," 73.

9 See also Motte, *Small Worlds*, who claims that Beckett "massively informs contemporary minimalist literature both in English and in French" (25). Beckett is claimed by both the Irish and the French, of course, but I would argue that it is his interaction with the French language and France itself that allowed for a reconsideration of his style.

The Passion of Martin Fissel-Brandt

Must it be? It must be.

BEETHOVEN

1

About half an ounce. That's what a robin weighs. Was that enough to tip the scale? What scale? It's an image. A picture. A painting. A cottage on a brook's bank. Never had Martin Fissel seen anything so hideous. Horrendous things of every type, in life, yes, but depicted in painting, no, never.

The robin is beautiful. Impertinent. Elegant. Refined. Sometimes completely idiotic. It had perched atop the painting. The frame. The top left corner. Had no intention of flying away.

Martin Fissel did. He had to. Leave. He had just spent a week there. Why there? To do what? Relax. Think, maybe. That's it. An uncontrollable urge to think. About what?

From a good distance. So he wouldn't alarm it. Martin Fissel. His full name is Fissel-Brandt. Motioning. Yes, gesturing. Not too vigorous. Not too animated. Meaning no harm. He'd caused it too often. Had been harmed himself. So often. As a result, no malice whatsoever in his movements, which sought only to convey meaning. To be heard. To be understood. Some impatience, certainly. But he was in a hurry: Shoo!

He spoke to it. At the same time, gently, energetically, he flapped his arm. He said softly: Fly away.

The robin was not moving. It seemed to have settled in. Its round black eyes. Two ebony marbles. Frightfully cold, stellar. Winter's black sky, in the night, stars. It was looking outside. Fern red in the front. The rest a gunmetal gray.

Motionless. It gazed at the uppermost tips of the pines. With each sudden gust small sulfuric-colored clouds freed themselves. Spring's pollen. It was springtime. In the year. It doesn't matter which year.

Perched atop the left side of the frame. Staring intently. Appeared to be saying: Go on, knock yourself out. As for me, I need a little time. To recover. Perhaps it was feeling dazed.

It had just thrown itself, head first, the impact was intense, against the kitchen window. It hadn't seen that it was closed. The glass was deceptive. It only saw the light. It was this jolt that made Martin Fissel stand up.

Until this sinister noise of a fragile body crashing, he hadn't moved. He didn't dare. He had told himself: If I go into the house as well, I'll frighten it, make it sick with fear and maybe, in the end, destroy it. He stood up nevertheless.

He was sitting in the garden. Eating his breakfast. He had finished. Tea, toast. Crumbs tossed onto the pavement. For the birds. One of Suzanne's habits.

He hadn't slept. Hardly. Poorly. Two or three hours in the morning. The sound of the ocean hindered his falling asleep. That sound and then. That sound like the breathing of some sleeping giant and then. That thought. Always the same. Which led to others. Always the same. The daylight reassured him.

It was nice. It had been nice all week. Perfect weather. Never had he seen that, such sunshine, back when Suzanne was here. His skin had darkened slightly. Every morning he had breakfast outside. Behind the house. In the garden.

From the first morning, the robin came every day. It landed on the patio. Next to the CD player. Martin had plugged it into the nearest outlet. He had left the player there. Near the patio door. He was listening to the first suite. Johann Sebastian Bach. One each day. Cello solo. Three in solitude. One writing. One performing. One listening.

The robin settled on the crumbs, pecked at them, flew away, and so on, that morning. The last. Martin had to leave. A Saturday. Came on a Saturday, he had to leave on a Saturday. He'd leased for a week. A bungalow with blue shutters. Which he opened each morning. The sea slept, low, distant.

God only knows what the bird was thinking. The robin, instead of flying away, skirted the house walls, with tiny jumps.

The patio door, because of the cord, had been left half open. It's not going to go in, thought Martin. It wouldn't dare. Yes, it went in. Dared. Martin couldn't believe it. He wondered what to do. Waited. A considerable amount of time passed. The bird wasn't about to leave. Martin was staring at the opening. A narrow passageway.

It'll never leave through there, he thought. It wouldn't think of it. A bird doesn't think. Doesn't retrace its steps. Because thinking is just that. It's cornered, imprisoned, trapped. It'll be drawn to the nearest light, the brightest, thinking it's the sky, and, since everything is closed, all the windows, I can well imagine what will happen to it. I've seen that before. It's a spectacle I don't care for. Try to help the animal and, in fact, the situation only gets worse.

Martin rose slowly. Slowly approached the door. Slowly, he pushed it. Slowly, indeed, but, when he entered.

3

The terror-stricken robin took off straight up. It was on the table. There were crumbs on the table as well. Spiraled beneath the ceiling like someone about to drown in a whirlpool. In the end it charged. Straight into the small window. Above the sink. A little square casement, painted white, full of light, of sky blue and pine green.

Martin thought: This bird is going to fall like a rock. One of those pebbles that, walking along the incoming tide, he used to take in his hand, weighing it then dropping it then rubbing his hand? Not at all. Hovering, static, the robin did an about-face, crossed the kitchen, and entered the living room.

Martin heard it circle, then nothing. Assumed it had landed. In turn, he entered. Looked for it. At long last, he found it. It was there. Up high. Paralyzed, as if stuffed. Perched on the painting. Atop the frame's left corner.

Martin opened the windows, the doors. After that, from a distance, he motioned. Attempted to make himself heard, understood. And even prayed to heaven, his God, that this bird would understand that he, Martin, only wanted what was best for it. Big deal. The robin didn't understand.

Weary, Martin stopped waving. Then felt overwhelmed by a great sense of despair. And, while still watching that icy bird, he was suddenly astonished that the painting was not moving.

Having thought this, he was surprised at himself for having thought it. Having had this thought led him to wonder: How, he asked himself, could a bird so slight and beautiful tilt a painting so heavy and ugly?

He wondered about its weight. How much could that little thing weigh? No idea. Say a number. I don't know. An ounce or so. Less than that. He waited patiently.

It was only after the robin's departure. It finally flew away. What had it seen? What could have attracted it so suddenly? To the point of making it decide? To give it the necessary drive to escape? Maybe simply a question of time. The bird's. Its inner time.

It was only afterward that Martin noticed the painting was slanted. Oh, not by much, I know, but still, it wasn't straight.

He stretched out his left arm. Straightened it.

4

As he straightened it. Martin Fissel-Brandt dislodged something. Did more than just dislodge something. Made it
fall. Something fell. Martin didn't see what. But he understood that something had detached itself from the back of
the painting, slid along the wall, and ended up behind the
sideboard.

He bent down to look underneath. Even though it was late.
He should have been leaving. He didn't suspect anything.
Of course. Assumed nothing. Simply wanted to see what
had fallen. Put the thing back in its spot. If possible. Repair. If repairable. If not then at least apologize, say well
then, I broke it, how much do I owe you?

He had to leave the house. The landlady had told him so. If
you could, before noon. He looked at the time. It was only
eleven thirty. Not a lot to pack. Sheets, some unused extra
clothes, clean, ironed, easy to organize, a second pair of
shoes in case, while walking alongside the sea, a wave
higher than the others, actually the tide was going out,
his razor, toothbrush, and what else? That's all. I still have
time. Oh yes, the little TV set I never used. Return it to the
back seat. Or the trunk. Yes, and finally. My CDs, my CD
player.

He stretched out his right arm. Thrust it completely under.
Dove his hand completely under the sideboard. Under

there, found some dust and a spider web. But thank God, oh yes, thank heavens, the spider was gone. On the other hand, there was this. This what? Hey, Martin, this what?

5

He thought he'd left. Acted as if. Drove slowly. He looked at
the narrow road, the trees, houses scattered in the woods.
That's what you do when you leave. Before leaving somewhere, you look at it. Or when people have to say good-
bye, they look at each other, one last time, to see, if they
are making a mistake. Heavy heart. Or light. Off we go.
About time. That's too bad. Already? You have to leave, already?

Being forced to halt. After only a short kilometer. Enter the
village, he entered. Stop in front of the house, he stopped.
Undo his seat belt. Get out of the car. Remove his sunglasses, speak to the landlady.

I found this, he said, interrupting that woman who deep
down he'd never liked. Already back when Suzanne was
here. With her air of not meddling. With what? Things
that are forbidden. What are you thinking about? Nothing.

What is it? said madame Jonc. Her name was madame Jonc.
Just like that. Nothing to be done about that. Jonc, Fissel-
Brandt, Leigay, what's the difference? None.

I don't understand, she said. I cleaned it thoroughly. From
floor to ceiling. Not where I found this, thought Martin.
She heard him think it. What's that? she said. I said: Not
where I found this, said Martin.

He continued: Do you know her, this. He raised the envelope to her eyes. Then took it away from her eyes. There, it's clear: This Sophie Leigay? Then lowered his arm, his hand, and, tight in his hand, this thing, containing he knew not what. Nothing, surely. May as well say that.

A yellow envelope. The address typewritten. Probably the letter too. He hadn't read it. Didn't even take it out of the envelope. He was tempted and then, I don't know what, respect, or fear. Maybe just tired of once again stumbling into a secret. Inevitably.

The stationery had to be yellow as well. A vanity. A woman's jewelry set. A woman's letter, perhaps. Or a man's. A man who liked yellow. Women. That one.

The envelope had been folded in two. Could it have been used as a wedge? So that the painting stayed level? Surely not. Even an ordinary letter. This one wasn't. What do you know about it? He hadn't read it. Why? I already explained. Refusal.

Even if he had. Just a note to tell you that I will arrive at Les Sables on the eight o'clock train. Or else, more briefly: Come and pick me up from the eight o'clock train. Even that, don't touch. No one has the right. One could be murdered for the eight o'clock train. Keep that out of sight. Let it be enough for me, he thought, to think that this message was hidden.

6

She one of your regular tenants? The tone is casual: Had she
been here recently? The last time was when?

Last summer, said Gisèle Jonc. Her name was Gisèle. That's
the way it is. Besides, Gisèle, Suzanne, Sophie, Anna,
what's the difference? In July, she said.

And you know where she lives? said Martin and adds: Oh
yes, obviously you know, somewhere in the Maine-et-
Loire, I guess. Why Maine-et-Loire? says Gisèle Jonc and
Martin tells her: I don't know, I said Maine-et-Loire because there are a lot of cars around here with license plates
from there, but if it isn't Maine-et-Loire, then good, fine.

He hadn't spoken like that for exactly a week. His last con-
versation was last Saturday. With this same Gisèle. With
the one difference that, last Saturday, having just arrived,
he was in a hurry to settle in, whereas today he was eager
to escape.

So? he probed. Where's she live? If I may ask. If it's any of
my business. I believe it is. From now on, it's my business.
Gisèle Jonc watched him.

Loire-Atlantique? he continued. Is she from Nantes? No,
I'm just guessing because I see a lot of plates ending in 44
around here. So? Forty-nine or 44?

Gisèle was uncomfortable. The inflection, the tenacity,
Martin's longing eyes, all of that worried her. What if he's
gone mad during this sleepless week of isolation? The

tide, the undertow, the noise, the sound of the waves like a gasping galley slave, in the night. Besides, she was haunted by an image: being murdered by a knife. Any other way, so be it, all right, but by a knife, oh no, Lord, no, for pity's sake. And it was almost noon. The tenants would be here soon. She had to clean.

Back when his wife lived here, she thought, I didn't have to do anything. She left the house in perfect order.

She was tempted to interrogate Martin about Suzanne's fate. She thought the word Fate by design. When a woman lives with this type of man. Perhaps he had. No, come on. What an idea. Ask him how she's doing. And your wife, how is she? I killed her, Martin would reply. Oh, Monsieur Fissel. You shouldn't talk like that. You don't joke about that sort of thing. Do I look like I'm kidding? Martin would have said, menacingly. No, tell me, do I?

You don't want to answer? he continued. Yes, she wanted to. But I don't see how, she said. Martin looked at her. He did, in fact, look quite threatening.

Listen, he said. I'm wasting my time here with you. And relax. I feel like you're afraid of me. Not at all, said Gisèle Jonc. Good then, said Martin. So, it's very easy. This letter, that I found, me, not you, I am going to give it back to its owner. If by chance it's on my way. So far, I don't know. So be nice, tell me where she lives. I'm not going to search the world over. If it's near my house, OK. If not, then, well, the story will end there. It depends on you. Go ahead, I'm listening.

7

It's none of your business. It's for me to deal with. Give it to me, she said. Then, a curious thing, she added: Have you read it?

And how! he felt like answering, just to shake her up a little. No. Of course not. Even in jest. It's too serious. He answered No.

No, he said, that doesn't interest me. It's enough to know that this letter was hidden. I have to return it to her. Give it back to her. I mean, directly. To mail it would be too risky. See what I mean?

Gisèle Jonc saw. She saw very well, in fact. What Martin meant. The same thing had happened to her. A situation with a hidden letter. It had caused quite a problem. She reflected on it. Remembered. Her husband came in. She heard him enter. Immediately quit thinking about it. She didn't want him to see her thinking about it. She thought he could tell. Having been caught once, she no longer believed in her ability to dissemble. Thought of herself like that, stripped of the ability.

Martin turned toward monsieur Jonc. He seemed like a decent enough man. Perhaps not so decent as all that. After all. What did he know about it? Nothing at all. Undoubtedly a hypocrite like the rest. He looked at him.

He remembered that monsieur Jonc, back when Suzanne was here, had had a heart attack. But he seemed to be in pretty good health. Questioned him quickly, about his health. How's it going? He was about to answer. Smiling, flushed. Gisèle kept him from it.

Monsieur Fissel, she said, asked me for the address of the Leigays. Martin caught the plural. There are several, then. At least two, he thought.

Do you know them? said monsieur Jonc. They live in Paris, I think, he added, looking at Gisèle. He had just returned from errands in the village. So, the weather was good, he said.

8

Yes, but where, in Paris? The rue La Fayette, I believe, said madame Jonc. Martin felt faint. He waited a moment. Took a breath. Then, getting a grip on himself. Hum, that's odd, he said. I used to live on the rue La Fayette, for many years.

He was lying. He had never lived on the rue La Fayette. He had simply gone there. For years. A building. On the rue La Fayette. An apartment. In a building. On the rue La Fayette. Number 7. He's had a bit of a shock. Him. Martin Fissel-Brandt.

What number? he said. Having asked this question, he fidgeted mentally, seemed to be saying: the rue La Fayette, OK, but number 7, surely not, not that, it can't be.

I'm not sure, said Gisèle Jonc. She was rubbing her chin. I believe it was 7. Wait, she said, I'll check. She was already turning away. Martin grabbed her by the arm. Hey now, let me go, she said, you're hurting me. Well, how do you like that? thought old man Jonc. Leave my wife alone or else. Or else what, poor old Jonc?

Are you pulling my leg? said Martin. No, tell me, tell me, are you by any chance pulling my leg? He had that look in his eyes. There were such things in his eyes.

Gisèle thought: That's it, I understand. I get it. I remember. He and his wife didn't live on the rue La Fayette. She sighed, then suddenly sensed that something. Something what, Madame Jonc?

This letter, she said, it would be better if you gave it to me. What letter? said monsieur Jonc. Gisèle looked at her husband, as if to say, carefully: Nothing, nothing, don't worry about it. He insisted: What letter?

Madame Leigay's letter. Forgotten last summer. Monsieur Fissel found it. That's all. He wants to give it back to madame Leigay. You understand? No, said monsieur Jonc. Of course you understand, said Gisèle. I'm sure you understand.

He's got a new car again, Roger said. His name was Roger. When I think what that must cost. A Swedish car like that. He went back into the house. They had followed Martin to the front steps. Gisèle lingered. She saw him fasten his seat belt. Put his sunglasses back on. He waved to her and drove off. She answered. Have a good trip, Monsieur Fissel.

9

When it's crowded you often say there's a sea of people: this sea was gray and blue. Smocks, coveralls. A little more gray than blue. There were more warehousemen in gray smocks. The mechanics in blue coveralls had joined them. They were standing around in little circular groups, murmuring. Question. What were they doing in the courtyard? On a Monday morning? At a quarter to nine? A strike.

Martin, in neutral, cut the engine. Got out of the car. Adjusted his pants. Fixed his belt, his tie. He sighed.

To reach the elevators, he had to cross the courtyard. No way of avoiding the strikers. The workers liked him well enough. That wasn't the problem. He liked them too. But this morning.

Didn't feel like talking. They did. They wanted to. They were waiting for him. To make him talk. The fact was that, as usual, they were counting on him to speak to the boss. Monsieur Lindqvist.

They said hello. He didn't answer. Didn't stop. A mechanic grabbed him by the arm. He turned. No, he said, not this time. You have to learn. One of these days, I won't be around to help you. The worker didn't let go of him. Martin shook his arm. Very well, he said. Let's go see. Sighed again. Raised his eyes toward the office.

On the fifth floor. Second window from the left. Mademoi-selle Lindström. Visible from the hips up.

She's waiting for me, he thought. She wants to know how I've been. If I'm OK. If I'm doing better. She wants to know. Know all. She's going to insist that I tell her everything. And them, there, expecting who knows what from me. Wages, quotas, showers, smocks, coveralls. Lord. Will it never end? I'll see what I can do. Would like to ask them: And you, what can you do for me?

10

Lindström was standing in front of the window. A charming person. Very tall. Majestic frame. Almost frightening. What do you mean? Nothing. Commendably put together. Puzzling face. A great gentleness in her features. Couldn't be more motherly. One of those childless women. More motherly than a mother. A sort of dreamed motherhood. Ideal. The benefits without the bother. Turning around.

There you are at last, she said.

I forgot: She wears glasses. Her eyes? Blue. A soothing gaze. A noncommittal smile, peaceful. And, a very important detail, no trace of make-up. In her pure state. Natural.

There you are, at last, she said. She spoke this sentence twice. The first time facing the window, reacting to the noise as the door was opening. A second time facing Martin.

He wondered what the problem was. With strikers in the courtyard. The boss expects to see me, I assume. Or else she was worried about me. She wants me to tell her. To fill her in. Why I came in late. No, more likely: what happened. The week, the weekend. The twist of fate. She'd never believe me. She'll think that I.

I don't give a damn what she'll think.

She'll think it regardless.

It's possible.

Maybe.

At any rate.
That's how it happened.
The bird, the letter, Anna.
Tell me, she said.

11

Saturday, late afternoon. The rue La Fayette. He thought he
would never return. Found a spot. Right in front. In front
of the door of the building where this woman lived, the
one that someone had written yellow letters to. Sophie
Leigay.

Got out of the car. Approached the door. In three stages.
Avoiding a collision once, twice, with a man, a woman.
Passers-by.

Hey, they've installed a coded entry pad. Just like that, they
confront me with a code. What am I saying? Forced it
on me. We'll see about that. He thought he might be able
to guess it. With luck. I am lucky, he thought. I've been
lucky. The letter in his pocket. I've been lucky. A space for
his car.

He closed his eyes. Gritted his teeth. Reopened his eyes
without loosening his teeth, then with one thrust dialed
96B4 while pushing his shoulder against the door.

Good, well, he thought, all I have to do, to enter, is wait for
someone else to enter. He was betting on a woman. It was
a man, who, on his way out, would allow him to enter.

The man had blocked the door with his foot. He was looking
for something in his pocket. Or making sure he hadn't
forgotten it. Time enough, for Martin, who had gone
back to his car, to get out again and rush over.

Hello, he said, then, pardon, excuse me, I'm in a hurry. Go ahead, go ahead, answered Pierre Leigay who, his reflections over, stepped onto the rue La Fayette.

12

Same street. Same building. Same light façade. Same door. But the floor? Was it the same floor? And, on that floor, was it the same apartment? Well, yes. Same floor, same door, same apartment.

No, No, he said, it's too unbelievable.

Not at all, observed Lindström. I myself, she said, knew a woman who had the same thing happen to her. And it didn't make her crazy, she, quite the opposite, it made her laugh. You should. She watched Martin. A smile didn't come. She continued:

Actually, she said, this thing happened to her son. He told it to his mother. Do you remember the apartment where we lived before we moved? Of course I remember. Do you remember my room? Of course I remember.

It was about a friend from the university. A young woman he had met and who, little by little, managed to find out that she lived on the same street where he himself had lived. What street, did you say? Ah well, that's funny, I myself lived. What address? Number 4, she said. Four? Well! What floor? I can't believe it. The third? I can't believe it. Yes, she said. Then he: Don't tell me you live in the apartment on the left? Yes, and she slept in the bedroom that he himself had slept in.

Well, then, I'll go ahead, said Martin.

Later, said Lindström, the boss is waiting for you.

13

Hello, said Martin. Is monsieur Leigay here? He just left,
said Sophie, why? What do you want him for?

Nothing, said Martin, nothing at all. It's you that I wanted
to see. May I come in?

This tall sad man reminded her of someone, but who? I'll
remember later, she thought, then answered: it's just,
you see, at the moment, I'm working. I'm in the middle of
working. You understand? No, you don't understand.

Yes I do, said Martin. What are you doing? It's none of your
business, said Sophie. What did you want to see me for?
But first, who are you?

My name is Fissel-Brandt, said Martin. He was ready to
speak. She closed the door again. He blocked it with his
foot. Not so fast, my pretty, he thought.

Pretty? Yes, she was. Even though. No. Pretty is not the
word. Beautiful, actually. A kind of latent beauty. Her hair
styled like a child. A dark gaze. Blond. A sweater. Only a
sweater over her skin. Dark gray. A low-cut V-neck. Long
sleeves pushed up to the elbows. Delicate arms. Light col-
oring.

If he wants to hurt me, she thought, I don't know what I'll
do. Call? Pierre is far away now and, on this floor, there's
nobody. That idiot below left on vacation. And as far as
the old crazy woman, she's deaf.

Are you going to hurt me? she said. Are you going to take

advantage of the fact that you are stronger? Of the fact that you are a man and assault me?

No, not at all, said Martin. What an idea. I only want. And I came a long way. To give you what belongs to you.

Did I lose something? she thought. You know, yes, that's what I'm going to say to him: did I lose something? she snickered, as if to say: what I had to lose, I've lost, so you see. Or even: What I held dear, one can't give back, so you see, your stories, the story you are trying to start, I couldn't care less. What is it that you want exactly?

He told. Tried. Began again. Summarized: to see the apartment again. Because I, he said, you can imagine, even right here, there where you are, I lived, that is to say lived, like you have no idea.

Peter O'Toole, she thought. That's who this guy reminds me of. I was wondering. And there we are. That's it. Happiness personified. She let him come in.

He stopped near the table. She draws, he thought. She draws for a living. She is an artist. Or an illustrator. Something like that. Or painter. Sculptor.

Is that it? he said.

Is what it? said Sophie.

You are what people call an artist?

No, she said. I am a musician. I compose.

Without a piano? I don't see a piano. Where's the piano? He walked toward the bedroom. Entered. She let him. A moment later, he came back out, a little drunk, his head spinning, from the sound of the storm, from the rain pounding on the roof, the wet bodies, the desperate bliss. Without a piano? he repeated. How do you do it?

I hear it all, said Sophie.

I see, he said, but then, that: what's that? Again leaning over the table. Over the large double paper. His arm outstretched. His index pointed toward the paper. Jumping from one form to another: what is it?

That's what I see, said Sophie.

Him: You see what you hear?

That's right, she said. The space on the paper is the space of an orchestra. The shapes are the sounds. I draw them. Then, I color them. Then, I translate them. I transcribe them. Into traditional notation. Each shape can be one or several colors. Each color is one of a family of instruments. Does that make sense?

I'm going to leave now, he said.

Sophie said: You do what you want. Every man for himself. Me, I write music.

Ah yes, he said, I forgot: you use yellow, I suppose. Yes, said Sophie, of course. And yellow corresponds to what? To the strings, she said, high, high-pitched, very high-pitched indeed. Yellow like this? Wait, he said. He pulled the envelope from his pocket.

I wanted to give you this. And then. Yes. See the neighborhood again. The street. The building. As for your living on the same floor, in the same apartment, I didn't dare believe it. But anyway, I'd hoped. Fervently. And it worked. Does that happen to you as well, to hope for something so much that it works out? It has happened, she said, but it doesn't anymore. Then he: It doesn't happen anymore? And she: I no longer hope.

The telephone rang.

He's coming, said Lindström.

No, said the boss, don't tell me he's coming, I've been waiting a quarter of an hour, he's here, I know it, in the office,
I saw him arrive, it's been exactly seventeen minutes, so
don't tell me he's coming. All that in Swedish.

Martin refused to learn it. He spoke and wrote English.
To him it seemed that that was enough. He stood next
to Lindström. Right next to her. And, even though the
phone was pressed against her white ear, delicate,
adorned with a tiny blue stone, he heard Lindqvist's voice.

He took the hallway until he reached the office at the end.
He met Jaouen, from Brittany, from north Finistère. Or
south. Martin didn't really know. Jaouen was from the
north. It was important to him that everyone remember
that. Martin refused to. This kind of stupidity exasperated
him.

How's it going, Jaouen?

And you, Monsieur Fissel? Have you seen what has happened?

Where? said Martin.

In the courtyard, said Jaouen.

I saw, said Martin, continuing his walk through the hallway.

A little further, he turned and pointed his finger, a long,
thin finger pointed at Jaouen's head, a small dark-haired

man with blue eyes and a trace of a mustache below the nose, thick wavy hair, with a part down the middle: You are from the north, Jaouen, right? Yes, said Jaouen, why? No reason, said Martin, then he knocked and without waiting, he went in.

16

In English, said Martin: please, speak English, he begged in perfect English. Lindqvist calmed down: Have you seen what is happening? he said.

His English was perfect as well but different from Martin's, mixed with something sickly sweet, languorous. Martin heard nothing but boredom there. A night that never falls. A day that never ends. Or a night. Nothing very forthright, at any rate. Where? he said.

Lindqvist looked at his secretary. Another Lindström. The same. Only older. The mother. Maybe. Smaller, she looked at Martin. Same protective smile. Superior. Colonial: Oh, these French.

Ah yes, said Martin, in the courtyard. Well then? What do you want me to do? I spend all my time making promises and you spend yours breaking them.

A smile from Lindqvist toward old Lindström: He doesn't understand, but that's normal, he's French. The motherly Lindström agreed.

Yes, I know, said Martin. The promises are made, etc., etc. The future does not belong, etc., etc. In short, if you want them to start working.

Nothing at all, said Lindqvist. Not possible. Not now. Speak to them. Calm them down. Make them wait. You can do it. I know they like you. They'll listen to you.

OK, said Martin, but on one condition.

Accepted, said Lindqvist.

Wait, said Martin.

Granted, said Lindqvist.

Very well, said Martin: that job, in Asia, I need it.

You'll have it, said Lindqvist.

Not enough, said Martin.

You've got it, said Lindqvist. It's as if you had it. But, he said, in my opinion, you should think about it.

17

But Asia, Asia. Where?

I don't know, said Sophie. She looked at a watercolor that the woman from before had left. She'd left everything. Everywhere Sophie looked. Everything was something abandoned.

As for Martin, he no longer looked. He couldn't anymore. He avoided it. Like music you avoid listening to. Until the day you decide to, and then that's it. Call it good. Not important. He wasn't there. He was: Where?

I don't know, said Sophie. Somewhere over there. She was thinking. The idea came to her that she should integrate a sequence in sextets. Two trios moving in circles. Approaching each other. Colliding then overlapping. Separating. She wrote the idea at the top of the double page. Sat up. Looked at Martin.

You know, she said. She didn't tell me much. Actually, she didn't tell me anything. But I believe I understood that it was near here:

She pointed her pencil over the large double paper, turned it as if hesitating about the direction to take, then moved toward the bottom right of something that could have been a planisphere.

The sweeping motion of her arms at first indicated: Suppose that this double page is a planisphere. The space is the same. The shape of the world isn't exactly like this, but it doesn't matter, empty the space and let's imagine the shape of the world.

18

He left. He was about to enter the stairwell. He heard Sophie
Leigay's voice. Wait, she said, then:

A minute ago, you know, I wasn't sure about what you said.
But now yes, I am. Well, at least I'm not far from it. And it
seems to me. I'm not sure but it seems to me. That. Yes.
She said a name. Her eyes were staring. Or lost. Or somewhere else. With a sad smile. I remember her smile. And if
I make an effort. I mean an extra effort. I could perhaps
remember the name.

At that moment Martin turned toward her. She still had
that empty look, avid, like a little flesh eater. Snakes fear
that look.

What name? he said.

A name like this. Or like that. Actually like that. Sounded
like this. She made some noises with her mouth while
moving her fingers, then: I wonder, she said, what family
of instruments, what coupling, or marriage, could make
that sound.

I don't know, said Martin, and then you know, names like
that, there are plenty, in Southeast Asia. Sophie Leigay
wasn't listening.

Pierre, Pierre, she said. Hey, what are you doing here? What
about your appointment? Thinking: It's obvious I'm not
going to get anything done today.

That imbecile never came, answered Pierre. We missed each

other. I must have misunderstood. Or, he forgot. Well then. He looked at Martin. This guy reminds me of someone, he thought. Are you going to introduce me?

Of course, of course, yes, goodness yes, she said: this man, it's the man, well, it's the man that lived here, before us, with the lady that left, anyway you see. No, said Pierre, I don't understand. Oh, said Sophie, please, don't annoy me, it's quite simple.

19

The cat waited for him under the awning, on the mat, sitting. The mat's thick, stiff fibers, close-cropped, poked its
rear.

It looked at him, as if to say: Oh yes, it's me, I'm here, as you
see. I'm not dead from starvation. I haven't been crushed
by a car, head smashed, brains on the road, or even, if you
prefer, my stomach open, guts on the road, and then later
the cars all drive over me, until I become a sheet of dry
skin, scarcely felt when driven over.

Filthy cat, thought Martin.

It carelessly turned its head then looked at him again: Leaving me for a week all alone, maybe you were hoping to get
rid of me, like you got rid of Suzanne, murderer.

Filthy cat. Get the hell out of here, said Martin. Beat it. I
don't want to see you anymore. Go on, move. The cat
stood up, hesitated. Dense strands of rain were falling.
Again, it looked at him.

Don't bother to give me any food, it said, that's fine by me,
I know where to find some food, but at least let me take
cover, let me stay under the awning, when the rain stops
I'll leave.

Go ahead, go in, said Martin, you're bothering me, but I'm
warning you, if you tell me again that I wanted to get rid
of Suzanne, I'll strangle you, I'll hang you from the ends of
your arms until you die.

He opened the door. The cat went in first. He followed it to the kitchen. It waited for him in front of the fridge. Move, he said, then he opened the fridge. You're in luck, he said, there's one more can. He opened the can. And, with the help of a fork, he dumped the food into a white bowl. Sound of the bowl being set on the tile. The cat plunged its head into the bowl. He watched it eat. It purred. It purred as it ate. It's happy, he thought. And me?

20

The light and the music woke him. In silence. The sun doesn't make noise. Music either. Only his memory heard it. He, not yet.

A moment later, completely awake, he heard it clearly. He heard it so deeply inside, it became so intense. He let it build. Emanate from him. Lips tight. Nasalized. Hummed it.

As he hummed, remembered when. Exactly when. Where and when. And why.

He had just left Anna. He was in the metro. He was walking. In the tunnels and he was singing Schubert. To help him walk. Simply to move forward. If he had stopped singing. He would have stopped walking. Would have sat on the floor and not moved.

He threw off the cover. Buried the cat. It slept at his feet. It didn't like to be buried. After a few shakes under the yellow wool, it reappeared, black, then, lifting its head, it looked at Martin.

No, he said, I didn't get rid of her.

Call it what you will, the cat answered. You killed her none-theless.

21

Anna had warned him. If anything happens to Suzanne. I'm
out of here. Immediately. For good.

Already, on another evening, she had said: Protect her. Love
her. Watch over her. Do for her what an ordinary man
normally doesn't. Give her all that you have. I will not see
you under any other conditions.

Upon returning. He found her. She was. He telephoned
Anna. She was sleeping. He woke her up. He could have
hidden it from her. In one way or another. No, he couldn't
have.

He called Anna to tell her about it. To not keep it to himself.
The ring sounded faint. It took five. She answered. He
heard: Yes. She spoke in her sleepy voice. It's me. Why are
you calling me? He spoke. He didn't have to but did. Tell
her. That Suzanne. She didn't answer. Hung up.

He found the Schubert halfway up the black CD tower. He was arranging his CDs. Took it out from its spot. Didn't open its case immediately. He held it in his two hands, in front of him. Put it back.

On the outside, this: Franz Schubert. (1797–1828). Quote from the composer: "I'll never trifle with the feelings of my heart. What I have in me, I express it as it is. Period."

Followed by a list of some of his works. The famous Sonata in A Major. Then a Hungarian melody. Then sixteen German dances. And, at the bottom of the list, number 7, an allegretto.

C minor. Length: four minutes and nineteen seconds. Hmm, it's short, thought Martin. How can I prepare for it? For what? For this brevity. To feel it all. Deal with it all. In such a short time. Listen to the entire program? The sonata, the melody, the dances? Wait fifty minutes for four minutes of. Of what?

He didn't want to wait. He selected, on the player, the segment. Four, 5, 6, stop, raise your finger. Push now. You hear? He looked, crouching in front of the stereo, at the number 7. Now, push. Play.

23

Anna Posso sat up. She was there, in the countryside. She sat up like an animal sits up. It has heard something. It listens, it watches. It has perceived this thing. Something is there, without a doubt still far away but there, already, not yet visible but present, it alone hears it. Nobody else has heard what it heard. As if she had heard something, Anna Posso sat up.

A river landscape. A large, wide river, deep and smooth. Layers of green marble drift along on the slow current. The veins are yellow.

She was leaning on her right arm, her hand flat on the pavement. She sat up when she heard. Perhaps nothing. She heard perhaps nothing. Perhaps it had only taken place inside her. A song. A voice. Perhaps simply a pressure there.

Something you don't anticipate. Or that you don't want to anticipate. That is overanticipated. That is so anticipated that you end up hearing it. She stood up.

With a push of her hand against the pavement, warm, leaving an imprint of her fingers, humid, she stood up in the aristocratic pose of an animal on the alert. Not fear. Alertness. In a watchful state. The steely gaze intently fixed on a strip of land beyond the river.

There's nothing. We don't know. Yes, we know. Nothing can come from that side of the river. Nothing concrete.

Nothing human. Except perhaps a thought making itself visible.

She doesn't see anything. She didn't hear anything. She simply believed. Or felt in her body. Or believed she'd felt something from afar that wanted to be heard, a thought chased away from everywhere and reappearing there, near the embankment where there's never anyone to be seen.

24

So, Mom, are you playing? It's your turn. What are you looking at? Nothing, said Anna, nothing. I'm not looking at
anything. I thought I heard something. It was nothing. I
didn't hear anything.

The younger one looked at her sister. Both of them
shrugged their shoulders and, with narrowed eyes, closed
mouths, lips pressed, burst out laughing, as if to say: She's
crazy.

Perhaps it was the constant presence of the children. The
obligation to throw herself into this ridiculous game. All
of it.

To move forward. At the toss of the dice. From one square to
another. Some character. Of ivory. Or animal. Of ebony.
Chipped. Beheaded. Or missing. Misplaced. Replaced by
whatever. A cork. A button. Anything stable. Everyone
knowing what it replaced. What value or what strength it
had.

The girls knew it. Anna, regularly, forgot. She wasn't dis-
tracted. She didn't think about anything. She was there. A
little thinner because of the climate.

Her right hand was placed on a star, with eight points, dark
red, inscribed in an off-white square, endlessly repeated.
An infinity of identical tiles. Calming at times. Dizzying
or frightening. Frozen surface. In the sense that it was
shiny, glossy. In some places reflecting. Warm because of

the feverish air. Separated by large green bands. A slightly dark Veronese. Empire perhaps.

The brief, intense state of alert having passed, Anna Posso put her hand back on the star and once again concentrated, made a show, pretending, her eyes lowered.

Ah, daddy, there's daddy, said Thi.

The beauty of yellow children. Extraordinary daintiness. Extremely delicate features. The eyes, the skin. Black pearls. Amber tint. Silky hair. Light, at the same time dense, jet black. Luminous. A subtlety infinitely multiplied, thick.

Each one had her bangs. Same style. Short bob, to just under the earlobe. Bare feet. Bare legs. Plain underwear beneath a short, white dress. Shift perhaps. Sleeveless. Made airy by the beautiful embroidered edges. Both of them. O'anh and Thi.

The younger one had a bad habit of running barefooted to meet her father, as soon as she heard the car. A vague noise, then clear. Then vague again, fading in a green thickness, the last bend, then coming back. Now clear again.

Don't move, Anna said.

One evening Thi was stung, or bitten, by a: A damn bug, said Michel Gaubert. This damn country. He said. This damn country full of damn things that: He was going to say: Waste. He looked at Anna: Kill children.

Three days, three nights, watching over her with a feeling that they had seen it before, lived it before, and then, on the fourth morning, she smiled.

Behind Anna. A dark wooden table. Some kind of sideboard. On the table, flasks, bottles. Syrup mixes, cocktails, alcohol.

Away from the table. Two rocking chairs. Facing the river. The rockers complicated by stylized lines, curves, concentric.

Anna Posso, Michel Gaubert, sat there, often sat there at length, without a word and rocking gently, their eyes moving from the river to the sky.

26

The plane banked, then traced a large circle. The pilot
wanted to show something to Martin.

At the right moment, while finishing his circle, he got his
attention by stretching out his arm, followed by a hand
gesture, index pointing, shaking, below, meaning: There,
look now.

Martin briefly looked at the pilot. As if to ask for confirma-
tion: There? The pilot nodded. Nodded repeatedly: Yes,
look.

Martin saw a wide line of red ocher, embedded in thick dark
green. Then once again examined the pilot's face, as if to
say: What is it?

Nothing but a wide line of red ocher, surrounded by the
rolling green of the forest.

27

When he landed, there was a car waiting for him. An old
Volvo model from the 120 series. Maybe from before that.
Before the 120 series. He had no idea. He liked it still. He
had almost bought one, one day. The very day he was
hired at Volvo France. It's been. More than twenty years.

They no longer made that model. You could still find some,
a few. He saw one once in the back of a garage. Navy blue
with red trim. Like the taxi that he took one night with
Anna, at the Place des Ternes, and with the twilight on the
Seine. They took him to see the company. He didn't buy
it. Never drove it.

This business about the car isn't interesting to anyone, he
thought. He still felt like telling it to the chauffeur. Just
to speak. As if it helped. He wanted to take the wheel. To
drive it, just for a moment.

What's the use? he thought. This car is one of the things that
I wanted, so? So what? There are so many things I wanted.
To live with my love, for example. He took a deep breath.
As if he were preparing to speak. To conclude or close
what he had just thought. Then sighed.

Tired? inquired the chauffeur. I'm OK, Martin said. Then
the chauffeur looked at him again. As if to say: So you're
Martin Fissel-Brandt? Then as if to say: What's a guy like
you doing here? The chauffeur was a nice young man. His
name was Daniel Stich.

Not a lot of people. Seven or eight people total. Eight exactly. Mostly men. One lady for seven men. Seven white men and one yellow woman. Four men at the left window. The other three men and the yellow woman at the right window. The two windows were open. Inside, on the ceiling, the inevitable fans were slowly turning like the propellers of a plane whose engines, clearly, will never start up.

You could see people coming through the door in pairs, then spreading onto the steps. With a relaxed pose. Not the slightest conviction of being anyone or anywhere: no one, nowhere.

With Daniel Stich on his left, Martin faced them. He asked them, with a wave of his hand, to group together, like in a photograph: Scoot together. This movement made each recall an event at some town hall or on some church steps. All in white, Suzanne was freezing. It was snowing. In January.

Because the two rows were even, Martin could only see half. With gestures, he asked the first row to come down a step, as a leader would have done, of an orchestra: one arm outstretched, the other bent, the left palm holding the second row still, the right index finger picking up the second: Please, scoot down, I want to see you, all, come on, hurry.

Situated in that way. He looked at them. A long moment. In silence. Hesitated a moment more and then. OK then, he thought, let's start over here.

I insist, he said, that, starting tomorrow, not now, it's late and I'm tired, but tomorrow, starting tomorrow, you will come in presentable attire. And that includes you as well, he snapped, looking at Daniel Stich still at his left. I mean nice. Clean clothes. The men need to be shaved, he added for the benefit of the yellow woman, clothed in gray. Turtledove. Slacks and jacket. Sharp and simple. Slender, medium build. An extraordinarily expressive face. Not serious, no. Seriousness itself.

Under Martin's gaze, nothing happened. The quiet encouragement he was hoping for. Nothing. Nothing in return, he thought. But it doesn't matter. I had to tell them something. I told them that. And, once again, he looked at the men.

They seemed completely worn out. Beaten. Or dazed. Distraught. Martin restrained himself from calling them scoundrels. Hoodlums. Derelicts. Happy to tell them this: I can see by your appearance, it's not difficult to guess, that in this organization nothing is working. I don't intend to go down with you. I have other plans, you see. At any rate, starting tomorrow.

What tomorrow? What's going on? Who is this nut? It was the voice of the foreman. He came in after the men. What the hell are all you doing there? What're you looking at?

He hadn't come over to the windows. He was trying to make

a phone call when Martin arrived. The men moved to let him by. He too was dirty and tired, but something distinguished him from the rest. His face, of course. His gaze. And then his legs as well. Squeezed into riding boots. His trousers were also for riding. Blond mustache and hair. A black gaze.

Finally, someone to talk to, thought Martin. Who are you? he asked when the foreman was at the bottom of the steps, facing him, on the same level as he, smaller, barely.

Delafontaine, answered the man. Philippe Delafontaine. People call me Dela. Very well, Monsieur Dela, repeated Martin. Now I would like to tell you, in particular, what I just said to your men. Is there somewhere we can talk? Follow me, said Dela.

Once both of them were inside, crossing the large, barely ventilated room, it was so hot, so humid, Martin following Dela told him: As for me, my name is Fissel-Brandt, Martin Fissel-Brandt. In front of him Dela responded: I know, monsieur, I've been waiting for you.

Let's pretend to play, Anna said. Let's not look like we're waiting for him. Let's act like we didn't hear him. Let's surprise him.

Thi, the youngest, once again, squinting, shrugged, as if to say: What a great joke we're playing on him. Oh my, yes, this is going to be fun.

O'anh, the eldest by two years, had noticed something in the undertones of Anna's voice. She wasn't amused.

In any case, she thought, it's always Thi that he kisses first. He doesn't kiss me until afterward. She runs to him and jumps into his arms. As he kisses her, he carries her to us, then puts her down. When it's my turn for a kiss, I can tell by his kiss he has already given all his love. Then it's Anna's turn, on the forehead: Did you have a good day?

We're not there yet. Michel Gaubert was still in his car. He had opened his door. He hadn't gotten out. His legs were hanging outside. He had turned to get out and, at the last minute, sat back in the seat and, leaning toward the dashboard:

He turned the radio knob. Not to turn it up. On the contrary. So that he could adjust the needle. Along the radio waves. To hear the news. Perhaps. The news of. Once again concerning. And doing so while rushing over the world with little one-centimeter jumps. He found a song that reminded him.

He was entranced, listening to it.

He got out of the car.

The tree, on the river's side, on one side of the veranda, a right angle formed by the columns and the balustrades, had, backlit by the setting sun, in its silhouette, something like a willow shape.

31

A wide line. Of red ocher. Dividing the green density. Seen from the plane, that was it. You could see it like that. Say to yourself, well: seen from here, it's nothing but a wide line, etc.

On the map, it was black. A slightly sinuous line traced by a felt tip.

The marker in his hand. The marker's ink, coupled with the heat and the humid air, released a strong odor, like a salve for wounds, first aid's wounded odor. The black tip touched the map.

Monsieur Dela retraced the line. He meant to show what existed. What was left, the rest, the end, was only a dotted line.

He explained. Commented. Angry. Took it out on everyone. Overworked the line. Retraced the line. The whole path again. On the map it's quick. A progression of several Kilometers. All that, only to be stopped short now.

A broken line in red, discreet, adventurous but not really, followed the thick black dotted line, some serious preparation had been done.

But tell me, said Martin. Yes, said Dela, what? He didn't budge from the map. Nor would he budge. Would not turn around. He knocked his boot with his ruler. A long wooden ruler. Used as a stick. Or a riding crop. That's it, he was lashing his right calf.

This guy is on edge, thought Martin. But tell me, he said again: you speak of this site as if you were responsible for it. But, as far as I know, we're here to import material and maintain it in good working order. Right? Am I wrong? Dela turned:

Who the hell are you? he said. Where did you come from? Who sent you?

Did I get the address wrong? wondered Martin. The wrong plane? Of course not. They came for me. A car was waiting. Perhaps for someone else? It's possible. At any rate, I got into that car. I liked that unkempt kid. Speaking of which, what about my suitcase? What did he do with that? It must still be in the car.

It's vital, said Martin, that the boy take my suitcase out of the trunk and leave it. Speaking of which, where am I going to sleep? We'll figure that out later, said Dela. No, no, right now, said Martin, I'm tired. I'll drive you, said Dela. But, before that. Was he going to tell him? Say it to him now, right from the start? He drew his attention to the map again.

32

Martin wasn't listening.

Are we going? he said.

Where? said Dela.

Well, to my quarters, said Martin.

Your quarters? chuckled Dela: Are you joking?

Oh, Lord, no. I haven't the slightest desire, said Martin. Even though, when I see you. You know what you remind me of? A British officer with a native revolt on his hands.

That's exactly it, said Dela. That's exactly what's happened. They massacred the machine drivers, and the machines, Swedish ones at that, supposedly indestructible, bulldozers, scrapers, loaders, giant trucks, graders, they sabotaged them all, you might even say, destroyed.

Well then, there we are, yawned Martin. Why didn't you say so? I was beginning to get bored, you know. Well, he said, I'm going to bed.

He wished him a halfhearted good evening. It was daytime. Hazy light, yet still very bright. He turned. Walked away. Saw the white men sitting on the steps. The yellow woman still standing. He stopped. Seemed to be thinking. Turned.

Ah yes, maybe not, he said, I still don't know where it is. Would you, I beg you, drive me there? Dela in front of the map didn't even answer. Martin yelled: Are you or are you not going to drive me? A voice behind him answered: Follow me. Daniel Stich.

In his hand he had, at the end of his arm, lopsided, shoulder out of line, Martin's suitcase, a rather nice, large yet light suitcase, in soft leather, earthy yellow with some slightly lighter spots, like lakes of dried sweat.

33

Coattails thrown back, hands on his hips, Martin, haltingly, made a quarter turn. His pose is one of an exhausted man who arrives in an unknown room and examines it in the presence of a third party, who put the suitcase on the bed: Tell me Stich, he said. About your name, do you pronounce it Stiche or Stick? Stiche, sir, answered Stich. That's good, said Martin, call me sir. But tell me, he asked again: What is the story behind this native revolt?

Stich raised his hands, then, not knowing what to do, he put his hands in his jeans pockets, near the rivets: You believed him? he said. Why? said Martin, I shouldn't have?

Stich shrugged his shoulders: Of course, I mean, I don't know: it's up to you to see, sir, he said, and, at that very moment, his thumbs unhooked from his jeans pockets, his arms fell down, then swayed as they dangled: Well, ok, said Martin, you can go now, I need to sleep.

Stich did an about-face. Headed toward the door. Opened it. Turned around again. Looked at Martin. Lopsided, nonchalant, annoying. Perhaps even exasperating. As if: Actually, I wanted to tell you. However, on second thought, no. That can wait. I mean, I'm not sure. I wonder. Maybe I should. No, we can see about that tomorrow. Finally saying: If I were you.

He wasn't him. No one is anyone. Martin himself didn't know anymore, so, once the book was sitting there, on the

nightstand, clothing in the wardrobe, razor and toothbrush on the shelf, suitcase set down on the bare ground,
then pushed under the bed, he pulled Schubert from its
case, closed the case, put it on the bed, then he plugged in
the little CD player.

He'd made up his mind. He would listen to it all. The great
sonata. The Hungarian melody. The German dances, one
of which is melancholy itself, and then, yes, go ahead,
press Play.

34

Anna Posso sat up.

Against the sunlight the balustrade looked like a row of ninepins set up on the edge.

Bowling is a difficult sport, thought Michel Gaubert. But what if on top of that. Stopped there. Told himself: Stupid thoughts always come to mind after the first glass.

After the second, he wanted Anna. He turned. Looked at her. He saw her sitting up. On the alert. With a worried demeanor. So elegant in birds.

She made a slight movement backward. As if this time the sound of the thing were closer. I'm not crazy, she thought. And then again, yes, I am, I'm crazy, I couldn't have heard it.

Did you hear anything? she said. No, said Michel Gaubert, why: did you hear something? Yes, said Anna, well, no, I thought. You thought, perhaps, you could hear me thinking, said Michel Gaubert. You've had enough to drink, said Anna. I'd like you to stop now. Don't forget that this evening we have. Yes, he said, I know, guests.

He started to rock again. Stopped. What did you hear? he said. I'm going to change, answered Anna.

He listened to her steps. Saw her leave. Imagined her steps. She heard something, he thought. Me too, I hear things. But I. What I hear. What I am starting to hear. Is what everyone hears. What you hear eventually one day. If you stay.

He poured himself another drink. He only had to stretch out his hand. Having turned to serve himself, he saw the rocking chair empty, without Anna. At least two meters between it and his. He suddenly noticed that there was always a lot of space between things in this country and, taking another drink, he began to rock again: sky-river, sky-river.

My goodness, what is that?

He sat up in his rocking chair. He too, had just heard something. This time something concrete. As concrete as a noise can be. In that it can be identified, yes. A sort of whining. It was whining. There was a whine. A bird?

Birds don't whine. Even in this country. Yes? he said, addressing himself to. No one. He spoke to himself. To someone. You say yes? he said. You say that in this country birds whine? OK, then, maybe it's just a bird. A bird from here. A so-called exotic bird. But no, it isn't exotic here. It's in its homeland here. I'm the one who, for Asian women, is an exotic bird. I prefer Anna. She doesn't want me. Apparently that was in the contract. No children, no lovers. Not even me. No, no, he said, not even from time to time. Nothing, so. Whereas I. As a result, I have yellow children that don't belong to me and for lovers yellow women and for that reason officially I drink, and he stood up.

He had, Michel Gaubert, still seated, placed his glass on the end table. Once standing, he stretched out his arm. Pinched the drink between his fingers. Brought it to his lips. And. With a stiff movement of his neck. As if caught in a vice. He emptied it. Put it down. Then. A pause. He looked at the shimmering distance. He had to cross the shadowy yet glistening veranda. Asked himself why. Why did I get up? Oh yes, that's it, he said. I got up to go ask her, to ask Anna, if by chance, what she heard, wasn't the same thing that I did.

On the way, he fell into ecstasies behind Thi. She was standing in front of this samovar sort of thing. She drew a glass
of water. Her left hand held the cup, the other turned off
the tap.

You no longer love me? he said.

He said these words as he gazed at the charm of bare feet,
bare legs, touched the black hair, then caressed the slender bare arms.

You didn't kiss me first, answered Thi. O'anh wanted to tell
me something in my ear, protested Michel Gaubert but
his voice was soft.

I know, said Thi, but I too, you know, I could've told you,
and so she told you? Perhaps, said Michel Gaubert: at any
rate, I have no idea what you, you would've told me. Thi
turned around:

O'anh wanted to tell you that while we were playing Anna
heard something. I know, said Michel Gaubert. And the
green plants, like this kind of samovar with a tap, set atop
a tall. Tall what?

I'm not sure, he wrote to Sophie Leigay, 7, rue La Fayette, Paris, France, if you will receive this letter, that's the sting of a letter. I'm not even sure if it will go out. That too, it's not without a certain charm. It would have been quicker to telephone you but the line has been cut. Yesterday, I assure you, it wasn't. Yesterday, when I arrived, because, yes, I must tell you, I have arrived. Monsieur Dela telephoned. There is something going on here, it seems, some things. I'm hoping for some extra help from you. On the map, where monsieur Dela traced his route, at the bottom right, I thought I could make out a name, which I will reproduce just as I saw it: PQTAM. It might be the one you told me about, where perhaps my love lives, you know, the woman from before, the woman from the apartment, where you live now. Tell me, please, if I'm cold or hot. I am only two hundred kilometers from that name, say three hundred, if I haven't, yes, misunderstood the map. I'm perhaps only, she's perhaps only, twenty or thirty short kilometers away. Yes, or two thousand, or three thousand, you're right. What did you say? I should check? Yes, I will, I'm going to, I'm going to.

Lord, he thought, I'll never send this letter. He dropped his ballpoint pen. A Sheaffer. Gitanes blue. Crushed his cigarette. Smoked them down to the filter. They left traces of nicotine on the ends of his fingers. On the package, of the same blue, a mini Bic. Then Martin got up and went toward the bedroom door. Opened it. Face to face with madame Tchaé, the yellow woman who, herself, was just about to knock.

She was all smiles today. Not happy, no. Joy itself.

37

Washed. Shaven. Combed. Clean clothes. Exhaustion apparent in their eyes, accentuated even more by their refreshed features refined by soap and razor. Showered hair smoothed out with a comb. It was worse.

As for Martin. Unwashed, unshaven. Had slept in his clothes. Looking at them, he thought: I am going to be fifty-five years old soon. And here I am. In front of them. Who expect me to I don't know what. On the pretext that I demanded that they. What do they think? That I am going to lead them to victory? That I am going to tell them: My children, we will not let that happen? Do not let those savages intimidate us? Let's go back to work and finish that road? The whole affair ending up with hurrahs and then, yes, hats thrown in the air?

How are you, Monsieur Dela? he said. Philippe Delafontaine had joined him. The two of them faced the men.

I don't see young Stich, said Martin. With his hands behind his back. Not looking at his neighbor. Never for a second taking his eyes off the men.

He was on duty, said Dela, last night. I see, said Martin, he's sleeping. No, said Dela, he's missing. From the roll call? said Martin, deserter? Killed, said Dela, probably taken and killed. Oh, this heat, said Martin. He took off his jacket and dropped it at his feet.

They don't want us here, said Dela. Who, they? said Martin.

The enemy, said Dela. I see, said Martin. Speak to them, said Dela. To who? said Martin. To the men, said Dela. Pick up your jacket as if it had simply fallen and speak to them. Tell them that we are not going to let them do it. That we are going back to work. And that we are going to finish that road. I see, said Martin. The whole affair ending up with hurrahs.

He sighed. Picked up his jacket. The ground was dirty. Shook it off. Put it on. Then, addressing the men:

Gentlemen, he said, I'm not going to, like a British officer, tell you, I don't know what, my children, etc.

38

Are you planning on staying there long? said Anna. I'd like to get dressed. She had only a long chemise on. Down to just under her bottom. Which was slender and masculine or almost. He loved seeing her like that. Michel Gaubert.

If it doesn't bother you too much, he said, I'd like to stay. That's right, said Anna, so that you can get worked up, and then you're going to be angry, and you're going to drink to calm yourself, right? Go on, leave, she said, leave me. To describe the pain Michel felt at that moment would take hours, without a chance of coming close to describing how he really felt.

As he was leaving, he turned: By the way, he said, where is O'anh? I haven't seen her. Where is she? With the maid, she's getting dressed, said Anna.

He: Why do you say maid? She has a name.

She: I know, but she's still the maid, isn't she?

Yes, he said, anyway: seriously, what you heard, did it seem like a whining sound?

Anna didn't answer.

He left her.

If all of this is true. If what monsieur Dela tells me is true. If they don't want this road. Then surely, my goodness, that's their business. If some of them use us to go against others. If they attack us as a way of disturbing the others, we can understand that, but we, we're not here for that.

No, no, murmured the men almost all together.

Louder, said Martin, I can't hear.

No, no, repeated the men, raising their voices.

At any rate, said Martin, what I think I want to tell you is that I'm not planning on leaving. I didn't come here just to have to leave again. Why did I come?

Don't tell them, said Stich. He came close by him. He repeated in a lower voice: Don't tell them, then stood next to him.

Hey, Monsieur Stich, said Martin, you're here? We thought you were dead. Happy to see you aren't. Monsieur Dela always exaggerates.

Come with me to the site. You'll see if I'm exaggerating, replied Dela. Where were you? he inquired, looking at Stich, as if to say: We'll talk about this.

Yes, Monsieur Stich, said Martin, tell us where you were. You scared us, you know, that's not good at all: go on, tell us, where were you?

I was walking, sir, said Stich.

You were walking? said Martin.

Yes, sir, I was walking, said Stich. And where were you walking, Monsieur Stich, said Martin, among the enemy?

You're kidding, sir, said Dela, Stich isn't.

Isn't what? said Martin. You're not answering me? Now listen to me, Monsieur Dela. Two possibilities: Either all of this is some kind of a politico-military comedy against a background of civil engineering, in which case we've laughed enough, or else the situation is serious, some of the guys have been killed out there, their bodies are waiting to be buried.

Emotion cut his words short. It showed him the sight of men lying dead over the machinery. He must have seen them.

If that's the case, Monsieur Dela, he started again, I believe it's my duty to require monsieur Stich to tell us where he was walking, considering that he was supposed to be on duty, right, Monsieur Dela, isn't that correct?

Everything was upside down. As if someone was looking for
something. Which in the end they hadn't found. Worse
than a mess. The tidiness of the room was destroyed.

O'anh was lying on the bed. With a dress in each hand. A
red one and a green. The crisp material, the bright colors,
spread out beautifully along her legs. She was on her back.
Her eyes surrounded by a chiffon paradise.

What is going on here? said Michel Gaubert. Where is the
maid?

She left, said O'anh.

Left? he said: what do you mean, left, where?

I don't know, said O'anh. She added. I said to her: Are you
helping me pick out a dress? She didn't answer. She left.
She looked mean.

Mean? Kim? You're kidding, said Michel Gaubert. And he
was going to continue when something brutally hit him
on his shoulders. A howler monkey. A bat. A snake. A vul-
ture. Such was his terror.

With a movement of profound repugnance, he grabbed it to
get rid of it, this thing that was attached to his back and,
not letting go, he held it in front of him.

A shrill laugh from Thi.

Then silence, fear.

She had never seen Michel Gaubert with a look like that. She
tried to free herself. She squirmed. He didn't let her go.

He held her at arm's length in front of him. I don't know what's keeping me from, he said.

He wanted to throw her on the ground. Against a wall. Wherever. Then had the reflex to do nothing of the sort. Instinct? No. A father doesn't have instinct. Threw her on the bed.

The bed sunk in, accepted her, then pushed her back. There was a rebound. After which Thi fell again on her sister. The two heads knocked. Thi's nape hit O'anh's forehead. Thi cried out, took a deep breath, and cried out again, and then began to scream.

41

The soft thud of bare feet. The star-studded floor. The foot's sole occasionally covering the stars' color. The walking woman was in a hurry.

Anna Posso hadn't made her choice of clothing for the evening any more than O'anh. She was still in a chemise. Bare legs. Bare feet. Her heels stuck to the floor.

When you two have stopped bickering, she said, entering the girl's bedroom. Then ran into Michel, who was leaving: Oh, so you're here? You're messing around with them instead of getting ready? Don't you think you'd be better off getting dressed?

Yes well, what about you? he said.

Me, me, said Anna, I'm quick, but you. Then, in a delayed reaction, she looked at the state of the room. What a mess, she said, have you seen this mess?

Speaking of a mess, said Michel Gaubert: I have to tell you.

Oh no, please, said Anna, not now. Go now, leave us.

So it was true. The ground was red ocher and the vegeta-
tion dark green. Monsieur Dela had only exaggerated one
thing. The state of the equipment. The machines weren't
destroyed. Only slightly damaged, and not really all of
them. As for the rest, he had told the absolute truth. Wea-
risome, fatiguing. Implacably recurrent.

The operators dead at the wheel. Heads tilted. Backwards.
Dangling arms. Or slumped forward. Had it been long?
Too long. It was time to bury them.

Question. What's the point of burying people so far from
their home? Aside from the decay? Aside from the smell?
With a cross perhaps? A plaque, a board, that no one will
read? Which, in the end, because of the monsoons, will
disappear? It would be better to burn them.

You can't mean that, said Dela.

That's exactly what I mean, answered Martin Fissel-Brandt.
It's like my wife, Suzanne, he added without apparent rel-
evance: What's the point of her being there? Reduced to
that and then. Well. She wanted to be cremated so I told
them: Go ahead, do it. But of course, you wouldn't understand, you didn't kill your wife. Speaking of which, Monsieur Dela, are you married?

He could no longer remember himself. He couldn't have
said to save his life. Under the pressure of an interro-
gation. If he had killed Suzanne. With his bare hands.

By accident. Or deliberately. But of course. He was so.
That night. So what? Can I say it? Of course. Unhappy.
That much? When he returned. After having left Anna. To
have had to leave her again. To have to always leave her.
That's enough. Stop. No, I will not stop:

She was sleeping. So he thought at least. So, when he saw
her, to make the pain stop, he wanted to. Yes. Suffocate
her. He saw her motionless and he imagined. Yes. Suffo-
cating her. And he imagined it so vividly that. And he realized, then, that. Only a small lamp was shining in the
house. Apart from that, there was nothing but silence and
night.

I'm surprised, said Martin, that he let us come here, come
back here. Then: Do you know, Monsieur Dela, what
they're going to do?

Who? said Dela.

The enemy, Monsieur Dela, the enemy: They're going to let
us repair our equipment. Start the work again. Then pan-
demonium once again. Rip up the ground. Tear up the
trees. Continue toward the river.

Oh no, said Dela, no, sir, not toward the river. This road
doesn't go toward the river. It goes north. Straight north.

Yes, whatever, it's not important, said Martin: You understand the deal, Monsieur Dela?

Yes, sir, said Dela. I agree. They're going to let us continue
and then. He shut up. Thought about what might. If he
kept it up. Incidentally, he said: no, sir, I'm not married.

Not all of the machines were yellow. The excavators, which
uprooted the trees, finished uprooting them after the
bulldozers had gone by, you could hear the roots groan,
complain, were red. Gaubert & Co.

44

The girls, under the threat of not being able to come to the dinner, had accepted, first of all: Are you listening to me? Look at me when I'm talking. To clean up the room, then to help each other get dressed.

Anna didn't know what to wear. I need to be comfortable, she thought. If the maid doesn't come back. I am going to have to do things. Serve maybe. For example. I hope that at least the cook. Oh goodness, the cook.

The problem with these large houses. If you want to assure yourself. Or to reassure yourself. You have to walk for quite a while. Or ring. A habit that Anna couldn't get into.

When she crossed the veranda again, something seemed disturbed. She thought it was only her thoughts, bothered by a question: Do you know why the maid?

No, madame, answered the cook. Thank goodness she's here, thought Anna. She entered the kitchen. Asking her question. Get the question off her chest. Put it in the cook's mind. Bother her with it.

She and I, you know, she added.

I didn't know that, said Anna.

The cook finished: I didn't even know she had left.

Now that you know, said Anna, do you have an idea?

An idea, an idea, said the cook.

Anna sighed: Yes, so, she said, you don't know.

Know, know, said the cook. She also sighed: It all depends on what you mean.

Oh no, listen, no, that's enough, you're not going to start too, said Anna.

Start what, madame? said the cook: if you came to torment me, I have things to do.

45

She crossed the veranda once again. Saw immediately what was wrong. The two rocking chairs were no longer parallel.

She turned. Came closer. Hesitated for a moment, then. Straightened the one that wasn't. It had moved. Some force had displaced it. Not someone, no. Or else someone who. No, no one would dare. Wouldn't dream. Noticed the hole in the wood of the back. The chair must have, also, slightly rocked. And, just when she stood up. Again. She stood straight. Preparing to. Something grazed past her.

Listen to him whine like a tomcat. She snickered. And, maybe because of the laugh, halfway between sadness and joy, her eyes began to water more than necessary.

No, it's not, she thought. It's not whining. He has a cat, it's true, I know, but. Simpering, yes, perhaps. Sometimes he would purr. Yes, when he rubbed against me. But apart from that. He wasn't like a cat at all. What could I compare him with? If he were an animal? What would he be?

Gestures. An attitude. His own. His voice. His eyes, perhaps. Oh yes, I see his eyes. On me. Oh, my God. How I would like it if he were. Here. If he would. Here. Now. Immediately. It skirted past her a second time. She jumped. It had whined a second time and, this time, from the other side.

46

The cigarette butt fell in the water. He fished for it. Not without displeasure. Threw it. In the ashtray. Sadness of a wet cigarette. The paper was torn. Tobacco all over his fingers. Rinsed them in the bath. A brief but strong nervous shiver shook him.

You could knock, he said, then. You frightened me, then. You want something? I don't suppose you came here knowing I was naked, to tell me you want me.

No, said Anna, I didn't come for that, I came, well, because: what you heard, what did it sound like? A sort of whining? Yes? And what would that be, in your opinion? What do you think?

I think, I think, said Michel Gaubert: oh, you're bothering me, listen, you have to know: from the very beginning I thought it was stray bullets.

Two of them, just now, went past me, said Anna. And a third in the back of the rocking chair. In yours.

He got out of the water naked, whistling between his incisors: That's it then. Sorry, he said. Then he immersed himself again. The disturbance caused a little wave. If you would get out of my, he said, I would like to get out of the. Then: I can't hear the children. What are they doing?

They're getting dressed, Anna said. Speaking of which: I don't know what to wear. What do you think?

He: I can't hear anything. I don't like that. Go see, he said.

A part of the tractor tread was damaged. Needed to be re-placed. A giant tire was blown out. The wheel needed to be changed. Windshield shattered. Take out the pieces of glass. Clean the instruments. The dashboard. And yes, it's blood, so what? The motors were fine.

One man's question: What should we do with Gaubert's equipment? Dela's answer: He has to deal with it himself. Assuming he hasn't died of fright. We can't wait for him. Clear that out for me. We need to move on. Start working. Where's Stich? Where did he go now, this time?

He was distributing the guns to the operators. Explaining how to handle them. The magazine, the safety. This one shoots a little high. Aim for the legs.

About Stich, said Martin, where was he, the other night? Did he tell you?

I knew, Dela said.

Oh really? Martin said. Well?

He's seeing, Dela said, a yellow girl.

Oh really? Martin said. In enemy territory?

No, Dela said. Not far from here. On the other bank. Over by PQTAM.

Where, did you say? Martin said. Over where? Could you re-peat that?

Dela repeated: PQTAM.

Martin felt sick. Very sick. And then worse. Cold sweat. Black
butterflies. He collapsed.

Stich! Stich! yelled Dela. Come and help me!

48

She found them sitting quietly. On the blue floor. In their
room. Facing each other. Silently. A girlish game between
the two of them. The youngest, Thi: a red ensemble of vest
and pants won each time. O'anh, the eldest: the same ensemble but in green, purposely lost. She always pretended
to let her win. They had put on makeup. The idea of future little yellow whores troubled Anna's thoughts.

You are going to do me the favor of washing your faces, she
said. The girls, at first, wouldn't deign to raise their eyes
from the game. I'm speaking to you, Anna said. The girls,
slowly, raised their eyes, looked at each other, then suddenly at Anna.

Well? she said. What's going on? Why are you looking at me
like that? Don't you know me? It's me, Anna.

The two girls leaned over again, over the game. With three
loud blows struck with precision, without pity, little Thi
cleaned out O'anh's rows. The latter, very dignified, nonetheless sorry, looked at Anna. Papa told us we could. Oh,
in that case, Anna said.

Are you playing? screamed Thi. Are you playing or talking to
her? You quitting? Anyhow, you lost. You're ruined. So?
You quitting? No, O'anh said. Very well, said Thi. You
wanted to. Go ahead, play. OK then, are you playing? What
are you waiting for? You scared? O'anh wept.

Anna grabbed Thi and, calling her a little brat, she dragged her or rather hauled her to her stepfather's bathroom. She was thinking: You could hit her, but she didn't. She threw Thi into the lap of Michel Gaubert. Deal with this. Because you authorized it. Clean it up. She left again, he held her back:

I have to tell you, he said. The site. Yes, what about it? It was attacked. He added: We are no longer safe. There was nothing Anna hated more than idiotic sentences. Her laugh destroyed Michel Gaubert.

There, it's over, don't cry, Anna said. Wipe your nose. Blow. Again. OK, again. That's good. There, it's over. Now, tell me. Do you know why Kim left? She has a lover, said O'anh. A young white guy that works at the site. His name is Daniel. And what else? said Anna. What more do you know? Nothing, O'anh said. She said it's far away. But he came to meet her. Ah, you see, said Anna, you knew that too. What more? Tell me. That's all, said O'anh. Very well, said Anna. Now, go see where your sister is. And tell your father to hurry a little.

50

Left for dead. But before that: What's the matter with him? Dela said. He was talking to Daniel Stich. Asking about the state of this tall man, blond with a face made of light blue eyes and a constant smile, teasing, perhaps. Even passed out, he seemed to be smiling, deliberately.

Did you speak to him about love? Stich said. Who do you think I am? replied Dela. No, Stich said, I'm saying that because, the last time I saw a man in this state, it was because of love. Or more precisely a deception in love. Dela turned around for a second. The men were singing. The engines were warming up. They were waiting for the green light. Yes, Stich said, he'd come up with a theory. Which was worth whatever it was worth, it doesn't concern me, actually I didn't understand anything. He believed that in love, if you lie, you are punished. He lied? You are so daft, Dela said. Help me lift him up. What did he say to you? said Stich.

Dela had forgotten. Dela was disgusted. Yes, disgusted. An unconscious man disgusted him.

So? said Stich. What were you talking about? Oh, I don't know, said Dela. About you. About me? Yes, said Dela. He had asked me the truth about you. He wanted to know the reason for your desertion. I told him what you were doing. Where you were. I told him about PQTAM. It was then that he started to feel bad. Where's the deception in that?

Oh, that's it, thought Stich. Gaubert's wife. The maid spoke
to me about her. When she'd had enough of me, she spoke
to me about her boss. It's terrible. She's going to make me
fall in love with her boss. Madame here, madame there.
Madame this, madame that. Madame is like this, madame
is like that. I told her: My word, you must love her.

51

Dela said: OK, well, what should we do?

Dela didn't know how to act with a man who was out cold. Whereas with a woman: you can slap her cheeks, you can loosen her clothes a little, grope her a little while you're at it, and you can fan her and, if possible, if you have some, if you are prepared with it, you can put smelling salts under her nose: Wake up, my darling, come on, wake up.

Night was falling. Lights lit up, motors running, adrenaline pumping, the men waited for the signal. Fine, then, said Dela, shall we? I would have preferred that he do it, but since he's passed out. Go ahead, said Stich, give them the signal. Dela got up, turned around, raised his arms, and the first bullet was for him.

Daniel Stich had slipped his hand under Martin's neck. He left him, telling himself: In his state, passed out, smiling, nothing can happen to him. Then he did his best to escape, jumping from right to left, in between the breaks from the gunfire.

52

So. Are we ready? Let's see. That's strange. Michel Gaubert
has made an old-fashioned type of collar like his father's
in the picture. Old from new? Yes. How? Well, he had
simply turned up the white collar of an ordinary shirt and
knotted a thin black tie around it.

Anna Posso, in front of the mirror, fixed her hair and was
speaking, saying: We have to leave. I am going to leave. I
don't want to be with them anymore. I don't want to be
with him any longer. I don't want to be here myself. I
want to go home. I want to be with him. If he's still alive.
Of course. He's still alive. I've heard his life. He's begun to
live very powerfully. I feel it. But I'm scared. Not because
the end is so close, near. I'm not afraid of that. No, you see,
what scares me is to be killed far from him, not to see him
ever again. That, you see, I can't handle, I would do anything, then: You're rambling, my poor Anna, it's too late,
so, she chased away all that, like an animal that, finally,
flees.

Michel Gaubert was less handsome than his father. Well
groomed like him. No mustache. On his father, yes. The
same fear in his eyes. It's there from birth. It makes itself
known. Personifies or realize itself. What causes it. From.
Yes, from the beginning.

They found each other. O'anh and Thi, Anna and he, in the
spot on the veranda where they usually dined, and it was

dark. Not pitch black, no, but early evening. The time when the guests normally arrive. They had set the tables. A large one for the adults. The small one for the girls.

The cook had done very well. The tables were beautiful. Simple and accommodating, casual. Sometimes they're too nice. One almost doesn't dare come too close. As with certain dishes. It's almost a shame to touch them. But, be that as it may, in order to dine, you must destroy. The lamps were pretty as well. Their light now dominated the natural light. Night was here. That was the most accurate sign. The only thing left to think about was the seating arrangements. Who would sit near who? And then. Yes. Who next to who?

I will let madame, she said, attend to that. Of course, Lucie, Anna said. One day, I will teach you. How to judge how people are. In what state of mind. When they arrive. And seat them according to that. Or, knowing them well enough, and knowing who knows each other well, thwart their seating plan. That's fun too. I'm going to drink something.

She walked toward the rocking chairs. What did she look like? What had she put on? Michel Gaubert rocked gently. A calm movement, thoughtful.

O'anh and Thi played. Patiently. Hating each other. They had chosen little horses this time to help them wait, to hate each other, to rip each other apart like hyenas.

Little Thi had, in addition to her intelligence, luck. Even

haphazardly, she won. Loaded dice, you might think. No, but. She had quickly learned how to throw them. She rolled sixes again and again.

54

She told him: You forgot to turn down your collar. He answered: I didn't forget anything. She was dressed in black. Her beauty, when she was in black, was for him, to him, unbearable. Let's stop rocking, he said, it bothers me. He was the first to stop. She didn't stop. Are you going to stop? he said. Don't get riled up, said Anna. She stopped, sipped, then rocked again, and went on:

Did you hear the thunder a while ago? I heard, he answered, rocking again too, Michel Gaubert. But it wasn't thunder. Oh really? marveled Anna. Well? she said. What was it? In your opinion? Explosions, I think, he said. The same as last time. And that, I admit, I do not understand.

Oh yes, Anna said, your story about the attack on the work site. He looked at her. Her dark beauty was unbearable for him. Turned away from it. He could have killed her. Gladly killed.

It's not my story, he said. I don't have anything to do with it. Oh yes, yes, you do, my friend, snickered Anna. He stopped rocking. Examined her. She didn't look at him. He pulled back his jacket. A meaningless gesture. The fabric snapped. You see that? he said.

He pointed to his pistol. He threatened. Continue like that, he said, and. She had that indulgent smile. The same one that. The one that the mother had. Michel Gaubert's. Next to the father. In the picture.

55

D. 915 in his head. Allegretto. C minor. Four minutes nineteen. Thought D. 915. Thought highway 915. Thought
road. Thought of Dela's road. Woke up. Came to his
senses.

Thought that Dela's road went straight north. Thought it
was Dela's road, not mine. Mine, which doesn't exist and
will never exist, not on a map, not on the ground, goes
southeast. He stood up. Brushed off his jacket.

Saw Dela dead. Was he? Didn't verify. He was. Martin
thought, that's the death he wanted. It's his road and it's
his death. Thought about the north road. Calculated,
approximated, a southeast angle. Made a half turn and
headed out, D. 915 in his head.

To help him walk, he sang. The allegretto sprung from his
head. Wanted to be sung. He too wanted it. To be heard.
Recognized. He sang. His voice was heard.

The enemy thought: Useless to kill him. They let him go by.
He sang at the top of his voice. Question. Why spare a man
you believe to be crazy? Do you think of him as already
dead?

Martin wasn't crazy or dead. He was singing, that's all. Not
happiness. Not sadness. Despite himself. To be simply
that. A voice. He listened to his voice. Wondered if he was
going crazy.

Soon, he wouldn't be able to see clearly. Worried about

his direction. Southeast. I should come to the river, he thought. Maybe, because of the dark, I'll even fall into it. I'd like that. It would wake me up. I'll swim. Not for long. I couldn't swim for long.

56

The Doverchains arrived with a burst of laughter. Two
  bursts. Two distinct laughs. A duet of laughs. One sharp
  and one deep. The deep one was from the wife: taller than
  he, a deeper voice than her husband. She and he, sharing,
  inside the car, the same joke.

Your lights, said Ghislaine. Turn off your lights. Marcel
  Doverchain sank back into his car. Turned off his lights.
  Then struggled out again.

Michel Gaubert didn't move. Anna stood up. She had to
  greet them. She waited for them on the stairs, in a twisted
  pose, patient, hurried, bust half-turned, quite obviously
  already tired: can we get this over with, hurry up and
  come in.

They advanced. Laughing still, shaken by some dying left-
  overs, remnants of the laughter. Michel Gaubert wondered why. Perhaps, he thought, they're mocking us,
  Anna and me. That often happens, things like that.
  Guests mock their hosts. As they arrive. Or as they leave.
  One saying to the other: I told you so. As always everything was predictable. We ate the same thing, drank the
  same thing, spoke about the same things.

They came closer. Their eyes were not laughing. Come and
  sit down, Anna said. Michel Gaubert agreed to stand up.
  He brought some chairs over. For that, a certain number

of movements were necessary. His coat slipped open:
You're armed? said Marcel Doverchain with a tone that
strongly displeased Michel Gaubert: are you afraid?

57

Get down, screamed Michel Gaubert. It was starting up
again. The Mauduits arrived. Their car had just entered
the property. Pof, pof. The headlights blew out.

Inside the car, Charles Mauduit and his wife, Isabelle. They
were arguing. About the situation. Which was deteriorat-
ing. They didn't agree. About what to do. Charles wanted
to wait. Not Isabelle. Charles believed that the govern-
ment would take care of the bastards. Rubbish, Isabelle
answered. It's more serious than that. Let's get out of here.
If there's still time.

The headlights had just gone out. Charles Mauduit didn't
immediately understand what had happened. If there was
a problem with the circuitry. Just a normal breakdown.
The dashboard had gone out as well. He was in utter darkness, braked, stopped. He waited while his eyes adjusted.
Then he noticed the lights of the veranda.

Michel Gaubert, face down, rolled over on his side, turned.
Anna had grabbed a child in each arm and had lain over
them. He could see them between the Doverchains' legs.
They were still standing. Ghislaine refused to lie down so
Marcel had stood next to her. He was trying to protect her.
He was smaller than she was. It wasn't even that he was
trying to protect himself behind her. Dignity dictated
that he stand next to her.

Well, that's just great, Charles Mauduit said, sick with fear:

how am I going to do it, now, go home, without headlights? He had leaned against the front of the car. He
looked at the lights as if watching them would change
something.

Something tells me you won't be going home, said Michel
Gaubert.

You can sleep here.

Not necessary, said Ghislaine Doverchain: you can leave
with us.

Something tells me you won't be able to leave, said Michel
Gaubert.

I told you we needed to leave, said Isabelle Mauduit to her
husband, Charles Mauduit, who was talking to Michel
Gaubert, saying: You drink too much.

Who in turn replied: I have an inkling, he said, yes, I'm quite
sure that the Lemoines are not going to come.

58

The cook had turned off the stove. It looked like they were going to have a cold dinner. She came in to see. My sauce is ruined, she said. She could see in Anna's eyes that no one gave a damn about the sauce. Not that Anna didn't care, but, my poor friend, if only you knew. And also, they hate it when you come out with that apron, I've told you a hundred times. I'm hungry, Thi said.

She had followed the cook. The big woman remained planted there, motionless, overwhelmed, a little red, looking like someone overcome by the heat of the stove. Thi squeezed her, then pulled on her apron: I'm hungry, give me something to eat. Give them some dinner, said Anna. I'll help you. She stood up.

At almost the same time, they heard a noise. A strange noise. Quite unusual. Even quite rare. A sort of rumbling sound. A sound of tires in motion, grinding up the dirt, crunching the gravel. The sound of an automobile moving forward, motor cut, continuing to move forward, maybe because it's being pushed, or because it has arrived.

The car, all its lights out, in its final moments, crashed into the Mauduits' car. As if no one was driving it. And, in fact, no one was driving it. Perhaps because, at the wheel, there was no one there. Perhaps because the driver was dead. The passenger as well. Probably his wife. In short, the Lemoines.

The others, the Mauduits, the Doverchains, followed by Michel Gaubert, Anna, didn't move, descended the veranda steps, one by one, and came to the car. Anna held back O'anh. Then she heard a voice. A voice that wasn't meant for her alone. Everyone had to hear it. The megaphone spoke, announcing: This is what awaits you, if you don't leave. After which, floodlights blinded them, then went out, leaving them even more alone in the dark, a dark more dark than before.

59

The water felt cold. Without a doubt he had a fever. He was shivering. Swam quicker to warm up. Had never swum before with his clothes on. The weight. Clothes saturated. Shoes. Lead. Weak legs and weighted feet.

Have to get rid of my jacket. He tried. Didn't succeed but it was as he was trying, having stopped swimming, that he realized a current was carrying him along. His horror of the water, of the depth underneath, turned into a fear of being carried too far, endlessly, something like a horizontal drowning, an infinite current adrift on the surface of things, perhaps in time as well.

What else? This. To have no idea of the width of the river. Struggle without knowing how long. The adversaries understood each other. Swim without knowing if. Swim nonetheless. Until exhausted. Don't think of it. Think it regardless: I will get there. Never will I tire. He remembered that man who had told him: I will never die. Who added: If you think that right up to the last minute, you won't die. He died anyway, but.

All in all, he was lucky. He was even doubly lucky. His aquatic drift, the current that was carrying him along, had corrected his earthly drift. He had walked too far to the south. The river had taken him to the east and thrown him on the other bank, haphazardly at a point precisely fated.

He pulled himself from the water, crawled along the bank, took a few steps, then let himself drop onto his stomach, but, sickened by the mud, made an effort to turn over, rolled onto his back. The sky was filled with stars. Everything up there seemed so cold, so harsh, so effulgent and cold. Perhaps I. No, Martin, don't fall asleep. Go. Go. Get up. Sing.

60

Anna turned around and looked. Not toward where things were happening. They tried their best to extricate the two Lemoines from their car. No, she was looking at the river. She was serving the children. Suddenly turned around and, from that moment, her face tense, she didn't move.

So! said Thi, are you serving us? I'm hungry already.

Nicole Lemoine. Jean-Louis Lemoine. She and he. Husband and wife. They finally succeeded in extricating them. The men were taking care of it. Not Gaubert. Mauduit and Doverchain. The women were standing behind them. Each behind her husband. Ghislaine was trembling. Not Isabelle. She was simply upset, very upset, which manifested itself by a stiffness that nothing, it seemed, could break.

But when Marcel and Charles succeeded in taking out the two bodies, the women helped transport them and put them on the floor, warm, of the Gaubert's veranda. I say the Gauberts, but these two weren't married. Anna Posso was Anna Posso and he was himself.

What's wrong with them? said Thi. Why are they lying on the ground? I don't know, said Anna. Yes, you know, cried Thi. Thi's tone was violent. Again that violence. Anna answered that they were tired. Or bloody plastered, said O'anh. Don't be vulgar, said Anna. They're sleeping, she said to Thi. That's not true! screamed Thi. They aren't sleeping. I don't believe you. You lie all the time. I can't stand you. They're dead. I know they're dead. Thi abruptly pushed back her chair and left the veranda.

She ran to the edge of the black night. O'anh followed her. They disappeared. Anna didn't try to stop them. Not one of the others reacted. Not even. No. Not even he.

61

He came closer to the Gaubert's residence. Moved forward, perhaps asymptotically, skirted the edge, without seeing it, then moved away further and further.

He was only three hundred meters away. After having thought of, dreamed about, the kilometers. Three thousand, then three hundred, then thirty. A simple question of scale. It was now only meters. The last. The last hundred meters. In the last ten or so. Then in single digits. Then the last digit, all alone, waited for him.

So, when he found himself in the dimly lit space near the veranda, he stopped singing and called: My name is Martin. I am looking for Anna. Do you know whether? If I'm near or far? Next to her or very very far?

I'm here, said Anna. Michel bid her be quiet. I'm here, she said, louder: I'm here! Be quiet, he said. Even louder: I'm here! Will you shut up?

Charles Mauduit came closer to Michel and Anna. What is this? he said. Then turned around to the edge of the darkness where Martin stood, muddy, hideous, half-dead: Where did he come from? Then again to Anna: You know him?

Yes, she said. With that, she left them. Stay here, said Michel. She didn't answer. He pointed his gun, aimed it. No, said Charles, no, not that, please. He held his arm back and Gaubert gave up.

Anna moved away from the lights. She made her way toward him in small, animated steps. Then skipped. Then ran. Then stopped right in front of him.

He sighed slightly, like a sigh of relief, then he held out his arms and pressed against her. It's me, he said.

I can see it's you, said Anna, silly. Why did you come?

I didn't want to, he said.

But you came, Anna said. Why?

Because, he said.

Because why? Anna said.

Because, he said. I would like us to leave. Both of us.

Where? said Anna. Tell me. Where to?